# The Secret in the
# Jelly Bean Jar

Written & Illustrated
by Ken Bowser

Solving Mysteries Through
Science, Technology, Engineering, Art & Math

RED
CHAIR
•PRESS•

Egremont, Massachusetts

**The Jesse Steam Mysteries** are produced and published by:
Red Chair Press LLC     PO Box 333     South Egremont, MA 01258-0333
www.redchairpress.com

FREE Educator Guide at www.redchairpress.com/free-resources

For My Grandson, Liam

**Publisher's Cataloging-In-Publication Data**
Names: Bowser, Ken, author, illustrator.
Title: The secret in the jelly bean jar / written & illustrated by Ken Bowser.
Other Titles: Secret in the jellybean jar

Description: South Egremont, MA : Red Chair Press, [2020] | Series: A
    Jesse Steam mystery | "Solving Mysteries Through Science, Technology,
    Engineering, Art & Math." | Includes a makerspace activity for hands-on
    learning about how to measure volume. | Summary: "Jesse's autumn break
    is off to a great start until she has big problems with her bike.
    Luckily, a bike is being given away at the general store but the catch
    is, to enter the contest, you have to guess the number of jelly beans
    in a big jar in the store. Find out how Jesse uses math skills to
    create a secret formula to solve The Secret in the Jelly Bean Jar"--
    Provided by publisher.

Identifiers: ISBN 9781634409575 (library hardcover) | ISBN 9781634409582
    (paperback) | ISBN 9781634409599 (ebook)

Subjects: LCSH: Bicycles--Juvenile fiction. | Volume (Cubic content)--
    Measurement--Juvenile fiction. | Jellybeans--Juvenile fiction. | CYAC:
    Bicycles and bicycling--Fiction. | Volume (Cubic content)--Measurement--
    Fiction. | Jellybeans--Fiction. | LCGFT: Detective and mystery fiction.

Classification: LCC PZ7.B697 Se 2020 (print) | LCC PZ7.B697 (ebook) | DDC
    [Fic]--dc23

LC record available at https://lccn.loc.gov/2019936021

Printed in the United States of America

0520  1P  CGF20

# Table of Contents

# Cast of Characters

### Jesse Steam

Amateur sleuth and all-around neat kid. Jesse loves riding her bike, solving mysteries, and most of all, Mr. Stubbs. Jesse is never without her messenger bag and the cool stuff it holds.

### Mr. Stubbs

A cat with an attitude, he's the coolest tabby cat in Deanville. Stubbs was a stray cat who strayed right into Jesse's heart. Can you figure out how he got his name?

### Professor Peach

A retired university professor. Professor Peach knows tons of cool stuff, and is somewhat of a legend in Deanville. He has college degrees in Science, Technology, Engineering, Art and Math.

### Emmett

Professor Peach's ever-present pet, white lab rat. He loves cheese balls, and wherever you find The Professor, you're sure to find Emmett— even though he might be difficult to spot!

### Clark & Lewis

Jesse's next-door neighbor and sometimes formidable adversary, Clark Johnson, and his slippery, slimy, gross-looking pet frog, Lewis. Yuck.

## Dorky Dougy

Clark Johnson's three-year-old, tag-along baby brother. Dougy is never without his stuffed alligator, a rubber knife, and something really goofy to say, like "eleventy-seven."

## Kimmy Kat Black

Holder of the Deanville Elementary School Long Jump Record, know-it-all, and self-proclaimed future member of Mensa. Kimmy Kat Black lives near the Spooky Tree.

## Liam LePoole

A black belt in karate, and also the captain of the Deanville Community Swimming Pool Cannonball Team. Liam's best friend is Chompy Dog, his stinky, gassy, and frenzied brown Puggle.

## Mr. Flemdrek

Owner of Flemdrek's Toy Store on Daniel Drive (see map). Flemdrek's has everything a kid could ever want—except for computer games. "Strictly analog here, kids!" Flemdrek says.

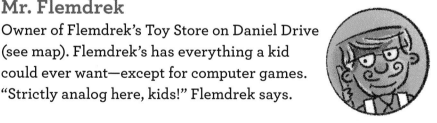

## Old Man Snord

Proprietor of Snord's Gas Station next to the park. Known far and wide for having soda pop— "so cold it'll crack yer dang teeth!" Oh, and free air for bicycle tires.

# The Ginormous Yucky, Messy, Sticky, Terrible Spilled Grape Juice Morning

# Chapter 1

It was the first official day of autumn break from Deanville Elementary School, and it was shaping up to be a pretty darn terrific day. Jesse only had to do a few chores before she was free to ride her bike and do all of the things that any kid getting ready to go into the fourth grade does.

"The first things I'm going to do," Jesse said to Mr. Stubbs, "are have a little breakfast, tackle that pile of leaves that I'm supposed to rake up out back, and then head to the park on my bike."

Mr. Stubbs didn't seem to be paying any attention to Jesse whatsoever as he gobbled up the crunchies from his bowl. He was like that when he was hungry.

Just when things were going as smooth as butterscotch pudding, the grape juice that

Jesse was pouring into her glass overflowed and covered everything, making a ginormous mess. Grape juice went everywhere. It poured across the table and off onto the floor. It splashed down over the yellow chair and then down on top of Mr. Stubbs' head, causing him to race across the room to avoid getting even more drenched in the sticky, purpley mess. It even poured down into the brown, leather messenger bag that Jesse took with her everywhere she went.

"What a DOO-FUSSSS!" Jesse scolded herself out loud. "I can't believe I thought that much juice would fit into that tiny, little juice glass." *The juice carton just didn't seem that full when I picked it up,* she thought to herself. *I guess I better pay closer attention next time.*

Mr. Stubbs sat off in the corner cleaning the sticky grape juice off of his fur. Jesse began cleaning up the mess.

It seemed like it took for-EVER, but Jesse finally finished mopping the purple juice up off of the floor and wiping down the kitchen table and chairs. *What a gross, sticky mess,* she thought to herself. *Yuck!*

Now all she had to do was clean up the fiasco she made of her messenger bag. "I can't believe it," Jesse mumbled. *I keep all of my most important things in this bag,* she thought. *I'm lucky I didn't ruin it all. I couldn't get through my day without my tools.*

Jesse started removing the contents of her bag. "My spy glass! Whew! Glad you're OK," she said. "My notepad's OK too, I guess." She set everything out on the kitchen table one by one for inspection.

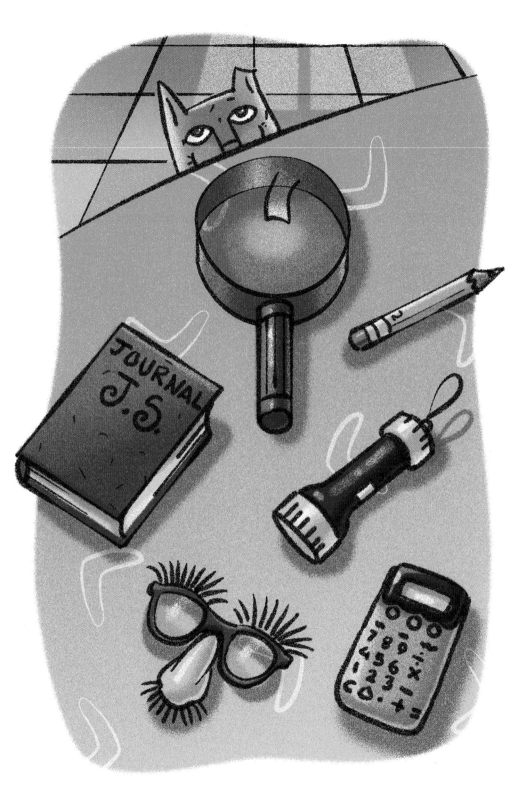

# Chapter 2

What started out as one fine day was quickly turning into one enormous mess. "I could just kick myself," Jesse mumbled as she was reminded of the disaster at the kitchen table at breakfast. "Well, at least that's all behind us now, and we can start on these chores. Then we can hop on the bike and head to the park, right, Mr. Stubbs?" Mr. Stubbs was still busy licking the sticky grape juice off of his fur.

Jesse surveyed the leaves in the back yard. "OK, let's get this over with," she said to Stubbs. "It looks to me like just one big trash bag should hold all of these leaves. Whaddaya think, Stubbers?" The cat stared back.

Jesse filled one big, green trash bag in no time and scanned the yard again. It was still covered with leaves. "Boy, I sure underestimated that, didn't I?" she said

to Stubbs. "Looks like I'm going to need another bag."

Jesse retrieved another green bag from the kitchen cabinet and filled that one just as quickly as the first one, without putting much of a dent into the remaining leaves at all. "What?" she asked herself. "Another bag?"

"How many bags is this going to take?" she said to Mr. Stubbs, who was now eyeballing the leaf pile with a mischievous grin. Jesse filled a third bag with leaves, and then a fourth. And then a fifth! She was piling up what she hoped would be the final bag of leaves, when Mr. Stubbs just could not contain himself any longer. He took a running, diving leap into the leaf pile and sent the leaves flying everywhere.

"STUUUUBBS! Have you lost your mind, you crazy kitty?!" she hollered as he played. Stubbs didn't listen and continued scurrying in and out through the leaves. He was like that when he was feeling frisky.

Jesse had to laugh out loud because leaves were now clinging to Stubbs' still sticky, grapey fur, causing him to resemble some kind of maniacal scarecrow cat. He had leaves stuck to his ears and paws. Leaves were clinging to his tail and to his sides—even to the top of his head. "You are one weird-lookin' feline, Mr. Stubbs." She laughed.

Mr. Stubbs finally settled down, and Jesse finished raking up the last of the leaves. When she was done, the two of them sat back and looked at their handiwork. There were now six full bags of leaves!

Looking at the pile, Jesse thought, *Gosh. I guess I'm just not very good at figuring out how much stuff it takes to fill something! First the ginormous grape juice snafu this morning, and now this.*

Jesse dragged the six bags out to the curb as Stubbs followed. Then Mr. Stubbs watched as she got her bike out of the garage. "C'mon, Stubbs," she called. "Let's put you in the basket, and we'll head on over to the park."

19.

An Exploding Bicycle Tire, the Great Jelly Bean Challenge and a Long Walk Home

# Chapter 3

Jesse was finally done with her chores and was glad to be on her bike with Mr. Stubbs. As she pedaled, she thought about the gigantic grape juice goof-up she had to deal with in the kitchen. She remembered how all of those leaves took up five more bags than she thought they would have. "It sure was an interesting morning, wasn't it, old Stubby boy?" she said to her cat, who was still picking leaves off of his fur.

As they rounded the corner by The Thinkin' Tree, Jesse noticed that the front tire on her bicycle was low. "Yikes. We better stop and check this out," she said to Mr. Stubbs. "It can be pretty dangerous riding around on a squishy tire," she warned.

Jesse pedaled for another block and coasted up to Snord's Service Station and right up to the air pump. Mr. Snord let all of the neighborhood kids use it for free.

"Hey, Jesse." Mr. Snord waved. "Do you need any help with that tire?"

"No thanks, Mr. Snord." She waved back. "I've got it."

Jesse kicked the stand down on her bike and helped Mr. Stubbs down. She set her bag on the ground next to him. "Let's see," she said to Stubbs. "How do you work this thing again? Oh yeah, I remember." Jesse had watched other kids use the air pump, and it seemed pretty simple. "We just press this thingy to the valve on the bicycle tire and squirt the air in until it's full." Jesse knelt down and unscrewed the cap on the tire valve.

Jesse pressed the air hose nozzle to the tire valve. It was difficult to put it on correctly at first, but once she positioned it properly, she heard it start to hiss as air began to seep out of the half-flat tire. She paid little

attention to the numbers, the instructions on the air pump, or the numbers that were written on the side of her bicycle's tire.

"Now, you just squeeze this handle thingy to start putting the air in," she said to Stubbs as he watched. Air began to hiss into the tire with a funny, hollow sound. The air pump began to ding as it measured the air going into the tire, and the tire began to swell. *Ding. Ding. Ding,* the air pump sounded. *Ding. Ding. Ding,* it continued. "How many dings is this thing gonna make?" she said to Mr. Stubbs. Jesse kept on squeezing. The pump kept on dinging, and the tire kept on swelling. *Ding. Ding. Ding,* the pump rang. *Ding. Ding...* and then suddenly, *KA-PLOWEY!* She put so much air in the tire that it popped!

Jesse sat up and brushed herself off. "Oh, great. Just when I thought my day couldn't get any worse," she grumbled.

"You OK, Jesse?" Mr. Snord hollered.

"I'm fine," she yelled back. "Now I gotta push this stupid old bike all the way back home. Come on, Stubbs. You can still ride in the basket," she said.

Jesse threw her bag across her shoulder and began her long trek home. Then, just as she started out, she noticed a bunch of kids gathered in front of Flemdrek's Toy Store. "What's going on, guys?" she asked Clark Johnson, who was at the front of the group.

"Just a chance to win a new bike, that's all!" he said to Jesse as she looked in the window. *A new bike?* Jesse thought.

"I could use a new bike right now." Jesse laughed. "What's the deal?" she asked.

"All ya gotta do is guess how many jelly beans are in that ginormous jar," said Clark. "The first kid to guess within 500 jelly beans, wins the bike. You can enter once a week, and Mr. Flemdrek checks the entries every Saturday at 9 am. The contest begins tomorrow morning!"

# Jelly Bean Dreams, Bicycle Nightmares and a Lot of Wild Guesses

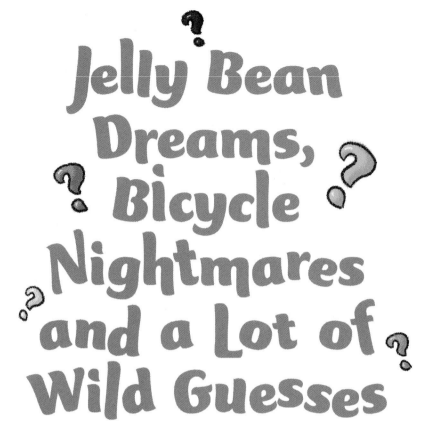

# Chapter 4

That night Jesse had a weird, crazy dream about giant jelly bean people chasing her on her bike, but the harder she pedaled, the slower the bike got because it had a HUMONGOUS, swelling front tire. When she finally woke up and climbed out of her dream, Mr. Stubbs was sitting there next to her pillow. He still had one brown leaf stuck to the middle of his forehead. "Silly cat." She yawned.

At breakfast Jesse was very careful not to overfill her glass again. "We learned our lesson the hard way yesterday, didn't we, Stubbs?" she said to her cat. "I know better than to try to put a half-gallon of grape juice into a six-ounce juice glass now!"

Jesse finished her breakfast without spilling a drop of juice and got ready to go

down and take her guess at the Jelly Bean Jar. "Looks like I'll be riding my skateboard to the toy store today, old pal," she said to Stubbs.

After cleaning up her breakfast dishes, Jesse pulled her skateboard down from her bedroom closet and grabbed her helmet and kneepads. "Not the best mode of transportation in the world, but it beats walking. Looks like you're going to have to sit this one out, old buddy," she informed the cat. "I don't have a basket to carry you in on this thing, and I don't want you out running down the street with me. Not safe," she advised him. "Sit tight right here until I get back from Flemdrek's. I'll be back right after I turn in my jelly bean guess."

As Jesse arrived, four other kids were already waiting. Clark, and his slimy pet frog, Lewis were there with Clark's little brother, Dougy. Liam LePoole was there too, along with Kimmy Kat Black from three streets over.

Jesse and her friends gazed at the huge glass jar through the toy store window. "I bet I can guess the number of jelly beans in that jar," Jesse boasted. "There must be at least a thousand!"

"No way, Jesse!" Clark said. "Look at the size of that giant jar! There must be at least a million jelly beans in that thing!"

Clark's little brother Dougy, who was only three, said proudly, "I think there are eleventy-seven jelly beans in there," and all of the kids laughed.

"That's not even a number, Dougy," his big brother whispered.

Kimmy Kat Black said, "I estimate that there are precisely, one hundred forty-two thousand, eight hundred twelve. And a half. I think I see a broken one right there."

"Right, Kimmy. Sure," they all said.

Soon all of the kids had written their guesses on the index cards that Mr.

Flemdrek had handed out earlier. "Kids, write your guesses and your names very clearly on your cards," he said. Mr. Flemdrek gathered up the cards. "Now, wait here a few minutes while I read them all, and we'll see if we have a winner."

Jesse and her friends waited outside for Mr. Flemdrek to return, all the while talking about how much they each wanted that new bike. Soon Mr. Flemdrek came back out.

"No winner today, kids," he announced. "Come back next week and try again."

"Oh well. I need to get home to Mr. Stubbs anyway," Jesse informed the gang. "If I'm gone too long, he gets into trouble. You should have seen him in my leaf pile the other day!" She laughed.

Before long, three Saturdays' worth of guesses had come and gone, and there was still no winner. During the last Saturday meetup, Mr. Flemdrek went as far as to say, "No one was even close. But think real hard, kids. I know that one of you bright, young minds will figure it out sooner or later."

Jesse had arrived promptly at 9:00 am each Saturday with her new guess in hand and left promptly at 9:15, disappointed. "At least no one else won the bike." She consoled herself. "There MUST be a way to figure this out," she convinced herself. "But how?"

# Chapter 5

Jesse was getting pretty frustrated with this whole jelly bean dilemma. She got a headache just thinking about it. Not to mention the fact that pushing herself around on that dang skateboard everywhere she went, had worn a gnarly, gaping hole in her right sneaker. Now, not only did she have a bike that was unrideable, her favorite sneaker was trashed, and her right big toe hurt like crazy.

*I still think there's a way to solve this jelly bean mystery,* Jesse thought to herself again. If she only knew how...

The last time she was at the toy store, Jesse had spent two hours attempting to actually *count* the jelly beans in the jar, one by one. She lost track every single time. "Arrgh!" she complained. "This is exasperating!" she moaned to herself. And even if she could count the jelly beans she could see on the *outside* of the jar, without losing count, there's no way she could see the ones on the *inside* to count them all.

On her way back home, she decided to walk—or limp, rather—this time. Her right big toe hurt more than ever, so she decided to carry her skateboard, rather than punish her toe for even one more minute, by riding it.

Then, just as she was turning onto her street, she heard a friendly, familiar voice.

"Hey, Jesse," the voice called. It was Professor Peach, the retired college professor. He lived on Byrd Street too, just down from Jesse. Peach wasn't really his last name, by the way—but more on that later. Anyway, he knew a lot about most things and at least something about everything else. Math, science, art. You name it. He knew about it.

So anyway, the kids just called him Professor Peach because his head looked

like a gigantic, round peach. Seriously. It did. He didn't mind, though. He thought it was funny too.

"Where's your bike? I haven't seen you riding lately, Jesse," the kind, old professor questioned. Jesse began to tell the Professor all about the *Great Tire Blowout,* as it had become known. She also told him about the *Ginormous Grape Juice Fiasco,* and they laughed. She even shared the story of raking the leaves and Mr. Stubbs' shenanigans in the leaf pile. Then finally, they talked about the secret in the jelly bean jar down at Flemdrek's Toy Store.

"It sounds to me, Jesse, my dear, all you need is a simple lesson in estimating volume," Professor Peach said wisely. He was always saying something wise. "Volume," he continued, "can actually be a simple thing to approximate if you know the formula."

"Formula?" Jesse questioned. "You mean you can teach me?"

"Why, yes," he said. "Let me show you. It's quite elementary."

The two sat down at the small table on the Professor's front porch. "First, my dear," the Professor said, "we must determine how many jelly beans fit into one cubic inch. A cubic inch can be represented by a small container that is precisely one inch tall, one inch wide, and one inch deep," he explained. "I'll demonstrate how to make a control sample." With stuff from Jesse's bag—a piece of construction paper along with her safety scissors, ruler, and tape—he cut and folded a small, square box just like the one he described. When they were done cutting and folding, they taped the small box together. "Now, I have a few jelly beans here that we can use in our test," he said.

The Professor began to place the jelly beans into the homemade container one at a time, counting them as he went.

"...fourteen, fifteen!" the Professor exclaimed when the small box was full. "Now we know that there are approximately fifteen jelly beans in one cubic inch." They repeated the exercise three more times with similar results.

"The *'equation'* for this, or *'formula,'*
if you will, can be expressed thusly," the
Professor pontificated. "The volume—that is,
the area or size of the inside of a container—
equals its length times its height times its
width," he continued. "Or written out in
formula form, V = L × H × W. We've learned
that the volume of one cubic inch holds

fifteen jelly beans," the Professor went on. "Now, on to the second part of our equation. How many of these jelly beans would it take to fill this?" the Professor asked.

The Professor held up a shoe box. "Next," the Professor explained, "using the same formula, we just determine how many cubic inches are in this box." The Professor used the ruler to carefully measure all three dimensions of the box, writing down his

results. "Now, this box," the Professor went on, "measures five inches by six inches by ten inches," he explained. "So our formula would read, V = 5 × 6 × 10."

Jesse used her calculator to find the answer. "Five times six, times ten...Three hundred!" Jesse exclaimed as she found the answer. "The answer is three hundred cubic inches!"

"Very good, Jesse!" the Professor praised. "Now for the final equation. How many jelly beans would it take to fill it?"

Jesse used her calculator again. "Let's see," she thought out loud. "There were fifteen jelly beans in one cubic inch. So..." Jesse put the numbers in. "15 × 300 equals..." She continued tapping, "four thousand, five hundred! It would take four thousand, five hundred jelly beans to fill this shoe box! Wow! Now I get it!" She laughed.

# Chapter 6

Jesse got home from the Professor's house with a real sense of accomplishment. "Thanks to Professor Peach," she said to Mr. Stubbs, who was waiting at the door, "I can now estimate the volume of a square or a rectangle in three easy steps! Whaddaya think about that, old pal?" She scratched Stubbs' cheek. "Next stop," Jesse said, "Flemdrek's Toy Store and the jelly bean jar—formula in hand!"

Jesse picked up her messenger bag, grabbed her skateboard, and off she went. "Back in a little while, Mr. Stubbs." She waved. "See ya soon, dude!"

When Jesse arrived back at Flemdrek's, there were no other kids in sight. After all, it was still only Friday, and the next contest drawing wasn't until tomorrow morning at

9:00. Jesse stashed her skateboard behind a bush. Then, to be extra safe, she donned her sleuth disguise. She didn't dare let the other kids recognize her and discover that she had a secret formula to help her solve the secret of the jelly bean jar.

Jesse walked right past Mr. Flemdrek as she entered the store. He smiled at her. "Hi, Jesse," he bent down and whispered to her. She went up to the giant jelly bean jar and got right to work with her ruler. She carefully measured the width, depth, and height of the big, rectangular jar. She very carefully jotted the measurements down in her notepad. The jar measured about 12 inches by 14 inches by 18 inches. So Jesse wrote it down in formula form: $V = 12 \times 14 \times 18$. Then she quickly left the store, whispering goodbye to Mr. Flemdrek. "You are one smart cookie, Jesse Steam!" He winked.

Just as Jesse was leaving the store and

tucking her disguise back into her bag, she heard the voices of other kids coming up the walk. Startled, Jesse accidentally dropped her notepad.

"What's this, Jesse?" Clark Johnson asked as he picked it up. Clark's slippery little frog Lewis was with him, as always.

Clark read the note out loud. "$V = 12 \times 14 \times 18$. What is this, Jesse? Some kind of secret code?" He made fun. "Why, that makes about as much sense as eleventy-seven!"

All of the kids laughed at Clark's silly comment.

"It's none of your dang beeswax! That's what it is, Snarky Clark!" Jesse snapped back at him as she grabbed the note out of his hand.

Jesse put her notepad back in her messenger bag and threw the bag over her shoulder. "See you tomorrow morning, Clark and company! We'll see who's laughin' then!" Jesse hollered at them as she hopped on her skateboard and left.

"That was a close call," Jesse mumbled to herself as she skated home. "All I need is the likes of smelly old Clark Johnson to find out about my secret formula and get a winning answer in before me. After all, he's pretty good at math already."

Jesse skated past Professor Peach's house on the way home.

"I've got the measurements, Professor!" she boasted as she waved the note.

"Way to go, Jesse!" He waved back. "Go get 'em, kiddo!"

When she got to her front porch, Mr. Stubbs was there watching from the front window as usual. "We've got it now, old pal," she said to Mr. Stubbs as she entered the house. "Now all we have to do is a little calculating, and we're all set."

Jesse set her things down and closed the door behind her. "Tomorrow's the big day, Stubbs," she said to the cat as he nuzzled her ankle with his cheek. "Now for a little calculating time..."

# See ya Later, Calculator

# Chapter 7

Jesse knew that she was going to sleep like a zombie that night. All of the excitement at Flemdrek's and all of the skateboarding really wore her out. What made it even better was the fact that her right big toe wasn't hurting so much anymore. *Hmm. Must be getting used to it,* she thought. She ate dinner and went straight to her room, anxious for what the next day would bring. "I'm going to march right down to the toy store tomorrow morning and win that bike, Stubby McStubbface!" she said to her cat. Mr. Stubbs was flat on his back, already zonked out for the night. He was like that when he was tired.

The next morning came gleaming in through Jesse's bedroom window like a big yellow ball. She leapt out of bed and headed straight for her desk and calculator. She began to estimate the volume of the big jar at Flemdrek's. "Let's see here." Jesse studied her notepad once more. "V = 12 × 14 × 18," she read out loud. She took her calculator from her bag and entered 12 × 14 × 18. The answer was an incredible 3024 cubic inches! "Yikes!" she said. "I would not have estimated that! Now to the last part," she continued. "We already know there are approximately 15 jelly beans in one cubic inch. So now we just multiply 15 × 3024," she said as she tapped out the numbers. When Jesse finished tapping, she could not believe her eyes.

"Wow, Stubbs! Check this out!" she yelled. "There are approximately 45,360 jelly beans in that jar! Holy guacamole!" Jesse said. "I would NEVER have guessed that! Gotta go, Stubbs. I'll see you in a bit," she said to her cat as she grabbed her bag and ran out the door.

Jesse was the last to arrive at the toy store, and all of the other kids were already

there. *Whew. Cut that one close,* she thought to herself as she skated up. *It's almost 9:00 already.*

Jesse wrote her answer down on the last card. As Mr. Flemdrek went inside to look over the guesses, they all stood patiently.

"I'm gonna win this time," Clark declared.

"No. I am," said Kimmy Kat Black smugly. "I have an excellent estimation."

Dougy Johnson said, "My guess is twelvety-sixty."

"Still not a number, Dougy!" They all laughed.

When Mr. Flemdrek finally came out, he had a big smile on his face. "Kids," he proclaimed loudly, "we have a winner!" A quiet hush fell over the group.

"Well! Who is it?" Kimmy Kat Black blurted, breaking the silence.

"The winner," Flemdrek said, "is Jesse Steam, with a guess of 45,360 jelly beans! Jesse's guess is within only 100 jelly beans!" He laughed.

The other kids cheered for Jesse. Well, kinda sorta. Later that day, she showed them

all how to use the formula for estimating volume that she had learned from Professor Peach. After all, she is a good-sport sleuth.

Jesse put her skateboard into her messenger bag along with her other stuff and got on her new bicycle to head home. She rode right by Professor Peach's house on the way and waved to him as she passed.

"Hey, Professor!" Jesse yelled. "Thanks for all of your help." She grinned.

"Way to go, Jesse!" He waved back. "Good job, kiddo!"

When Jesse got home, she put Mr. Stubbs in the front basket of her new bike and took him for a long ride through the neighborhood. He purred and smiled. As she pedaled, he closed his green eyes and sniffed at the air. He was like that when he was happy.

THE END

# Jesse's Word List

**Accomplishment**
something that you finished—like a doughnut

**Difficult**
when something is really hard to do—like
spelling pterodactyl

**Dilemma**
a big problem—like if your dog ate your homework

**Enormous**
something big—like the mistake I made when
I tried to spell pterodactyl

**Fiasco**
really screwing something up badly

**Ginormous**
really, really, really, really, really big

**Guacamole**
that green glop that some people put on their tacos

**Humongous**
even bigger than ginormous

**Mischievous**
causing trouble—*I was being mischievous
when I dumped grape juice on my sister's head.*

**Pontificated**
explained something like you're a smarty-pants

**Shenanigans**
goofing around like a dork

**Snafu**
a big mess—*I created a snafu when I dumped the grape juice on my sister's head.*

**Surveyed**
looked at something really close with your eyeballs

**Underestimated**
an estimate that is too low—*I underestimated the trouble I'd get in to when I dumped the grape juice on my sister's head.*

## About the Author & Illustrator

**Ken Bowser** is an illustrator and writer whose work has appeared in hundreds of books and countless periodicals. While he's been drawing for as long as he could hold a pencil, all of his work today is created digitally on a computer. He works out of his home studio in Central Florida with his wife Laura and a big, lazy, orange cat.

# Try It Out!

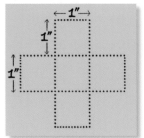

1. Begin with small, equally-sized objects, like jelly beans. Other things that would also work that you might have around the house are dried beans or unpopped popcorn.

2. Make a small box with construction paper, safety scissors, and a ruler (see diagram). Now determine how many of the objects fit in the one cubic inch.

3. Next, find a larger square or rectangular box or container (like a shoe box). Measure all sides of the larger container. Now using the formula Volume = Length × Height × Width, or $V = L \times H \times W$, and your math skills or calculator, estimate the total square inches in the box and how many of the small objects it would take to fill the big container.

4. Note: you don't have to fill the big box. It's fun enough to know how many would be needed to fill it!